Randolph T. Percy

**Who Was G. W.?**

being a truthful tale of the Seventh regiment in the armory, during the

railroad strikes in July, 1877

Randolph T. Percy

**Who Was G. W.?**
*being a truthful tale of the Seventh regiment in the armory, during the railroad strikes in July, 1877*

ISBN/EAN: 9783337154349

Printed in Europe, USA, Canada, Australia, Japan

Cover: Foto ©Andreas Hilbeck / pixelio.de

More available books at **www.hansebooks.com**

# "WHO WAS G. W.?"

"OUT OF THE WORLD" SERIES No. IV.

♦

# "WHO WAS G. W.?"

BEING

## A TRUTHFUL TALE

OF

## The Seventh Regiment in the Armory, during the Railroad Strikes in July, 1877.

♦

*REPRINTED FROM "THE WORLD."*

NEW-YORK: 1879.

[NOTE.—The following history appears here substantially as it was printed in THE WORLD, with the addition of a prologue and such few alterations as were necessary to avoid breaking the continuity of the narrative.]

# CONTENTS.

# PROLOGUE.

"J'AIME LE MILITAIRE," sang Phillis gaily, with plumes of cardinal flower nodding quaintly in her hat, and marching firmly up and down the bank, where I lay looking at the ripples on the lake, and watching the little patches of sunshine flickering down between the leaves and dancing on the grass.

"You have good reason for that. Better than you have for most of your likes and dislikes, at least," growled the family Mentor from a post on the rocks above, where he sat, looking like the "lone fisherman."

" Because —— ? " interrogated Phillis.

" Because," echoes the Mentor. " You landed Jack there, all because he was 'spooney' and plunged over the brink,— where he had been hovering for weeks,— the night he was sent for to join his regiment, when the railroad men struck, last year."

" Yes, I think that did have something to do with it," replied Phillis demurely; " but then you see," with sudden inspiration, " he was sure to have done it some time or other. Were n't you, Jack ? "

I grin, and shy a stone into the lake, without replying.

" I hate engaged men," says the Mentor viciously. " They are always like Mohammed's coffin, suspended between heaven and earth. Having rashly abjured bachelor privileges and divertisements, and not yet having attained to the delights of married life, they are the most miserable creatures in existence. Pah ! "

"It's a blessing that we don't know what pitiable wretches we are," I exclaim.

"Jack," says Phillis, "tell me again all about Camp Hardscrabble. I like to hear it."

"Oh Lord! He thinks that story is part of his romance. I decline to hear it again;" and the Mentor disappears in the primeval forest. Reader, you may accompany the wise Mentor and make your escape into the woods, or stay with Phillis and hear my story. This is it.

# I.

"Are not you moved, when all the sway of Earth
Shakes like a thing unfirm?"

JULIUS CÆSAR.

THE anxiety and apprehension which pervaded New-York City on Monday morning, the 23d of July, 1877, were greater than they had ever been since the dread days in the summer of 1863, when the city was actually powerless in the hands of a mob.

Thousands of railroad employés in various parts of the country had struck work, and were being joined at the most eligible points by a vast army of tramps who were eager to share in the plunder which might accrue from the acts of violence and pillage to which demagogues sought to incite the strikers. Railroad and mail communication between the East and West was entirely suspended; the great trunk lines were in the hands of the mob of strikers at most important points, and in some cases the telegraph lines were down. There had been violence and bloodshed in other cities, and at Pittsburg the collision between the mob and the militia had resulted in the rout of the latter.

The red flag of the Commune had been raised in New-York, inflammatory proclamations printed and circulated, and a mass meeting called in Tompkins Square for Wednesday night. There was good reason to fear the result of bringing together so much inflammable material to be exposed to the firebrands which demagogues were preparing to hurl in its midst.

Added to this, there came the startling thought into many minds that a leader might be found for these disorganized mobs who would lead them to avail themselves of their manifest advantage in having virtually cut the country in two, and thus enable them to remain masters of the situation.

That these were not idle fears, men were assured of by the fact that the President of the United States had called around him his Cabinet, and that they had seriously considered the extreme measure of a suspension of the habeas corpus. This action was postponed for a day, and the President issued a proclamation preparatory to declaring martial law in several of the States where the insurrection was most formidable. The Secretaries of War and of the Navy began to prepare for more serious possibilities. Military and naval stores were hastily prepared, and the commanders of the forces, by land and sea, received telegraphic orders to hold themselves in readiness for immediate service.

Meanwhile, business was almost entirely suspended, and the members of the business community, in their enforced idleness, could only seek eagerly for the latest news, and discuss the situation with gloomy forebodings. Men were thankful that their families were safely located in the quietude of the country, and those whose families were in the city instructed them to remain at home. The streets were almost entirely deserted, and the broiling July sun lay along the sidewalks unbroken by the usual passing shadows.

At four o'clock in the afternoon of that day, Adjutant-General Townsend received the following dispatch at his head-quarters in Albany, from Oneonta, N. Y. :

I am on my way to Albany. You will direct the major-general of each division in the State to hold his command in readiness for service at a moment's notice, subject to my orders.

(Signed) L. ROBINSON, Governor.

When this announcement reached the city, coupled with the declaration of the

Governor that he would, if necessary, call for 100,000 volunteers, in addition to the 28,000 members of the National Guard, a revulsion of public feeling was at once experienced. The confidence of the people of the city in their crack regiments was always unbounded, and they began to have a returning confidence in the speedy triumph of the law, when it was backed by bayonets.

The Adjutant-General, through his assistant, Colonel Alfred H. Taylor, immediately transmitted the Governor's order by telegraph to the head-quarters of the division commanders throughout the State. The following was received at the head-quarters of the First Division:

*Major-General Alexander Shaler, Commanding First Division, N. G. S. N. Y., No. 155 Mercer Street:*

The Commander-in-Chief directs that you have your entire command ready for service, and hold them subject to his orders.

FRANKLIN TOWNSEND,
Adjutant-General.

2

Colonel Carl Jussen, Division Inspector and Acting Assistant Adjutant-General to General Shaler, at once prepared the following, which was issued at 4.55 P. M. :

HEAD-QUARTERS FIRST DIVISION, }
N. G. S. N. Y., }
New-York, July 23, 1877. }

General Orders, No. 6.

In obedience to orders from the Commander-in-Chief. the division will assemble, armed and fully equipped, at the armories of the several organizations without delay.

By order of Major-General Alexander Shaler.

CARL JUSSEN,
Colonel and Division Inspector.

By telegraph and special messenger the orders were very promptly carried to the several armories, as well as to the residences of the colonels and commanding officers. By 7 o'clock the news had become generally known, and the men poured into the armories at a lively rate.

During the entire evening soldiers in uniform and others bearing soldierly accouterments filled the streets which had been so nearly deserted all day. Occasionally a cheer would greet a passing group of the Seventh's boys, and again a suppressed murmur of disapproval would go up, but neither interfered with their hastily seeking the armory in Tompkins Market.

Here even those who arrived earliest found that the call for the assembling of the regiment had been anticipated by Colonel Emmons Clark, who had issued an order during the afternoon for the assembling of a guard of fifty men at the armory. This was done in accordance with his invariable custom at times when great excitement prevails in the city, in order that no person shall obtain from the armory any arms or ammunition by force or otherwise. The wisdom of this action was seen at once in that Colonel Clark, when he reached the armory, had already at his hand fifty men to be used as a guard and in notifying the members

of the regiment that they were wanted.
The first movement made was to send for
two howitzers which belong to the regiment but which had been for some time
lying in the State Arsenal, and they were
at once placed in position to command
the entrance to the armory. A lieutenant
of the Second Company, who was officer
of the guard, immediately sent out messengers in search of the members of the
regiment, and they began to come in at
once. As fast as the non-commissioned
officers arrived they were posted off in
hot haste to notify the men, who then
began to arrive in numbers. The guard
placed over the doors was quadrupled as
the crowd collected in the street outside,
and strict orders were given that no one
should be admitted to the armory except
the members of the regiment and of the
veteran corps. The men hastened to
don their uniforms, many of them putting
on their knapsacks and getting ready for

active service at once. They soon discarded again everything but their shirts—it was hot. Still, the men kept coming, many of them bringing large traveling-bags, and evidently prepared to stay in the armory or go anywhere else for an indefinite period. The members of the veteran corps came to the front almost as promptly as the active members, and not a few white haired and mustached veterans donned their uniforms and prepared for the fray. Queries as to what they were to do or where to go were on every man's tongue. Meanwhile the friends of the members who had accompanied them to the armory and were unable to gain admission, and the idlers and others attracted to the spot to the number of several hundred, effectually blockaded the street, and the captain of the Seventeenth Police Precinct appeared on the scene at 10.30 with a file of reserves, and cleared the street without the slightest opposition.

At 11 o'clock nearly 500 men were assembled in the armory, and telegrams were being received from men out of town, all of whom were coming by first train, so that it was expected 1,000 men of the active and veteran organizations would be on hand by 10 A. M. the following day. The boys started a piano going in one of the company rooms, and glees and carols were given lustily, but the more phlegmatic men, taking their overcoats for pillows, stretched themselves on the floor and on benches to sleep, saying, "If they had work to do, they'd need it, and if not it couldn't hurt them."

But their slumbers were not undisturbed by any means, for all night long perturbed spirits walked the night in light and airy attire, and mischievous ones began to give indications of the carnival of fun which was soon to be inaugurated.

The stillness of midnight which fell upon the streets, as nearly deserted as the

streets of a metropolitan city ever are,
made audible throughout the armory the
clatter of hoofs as some non-commissioned
officer, transformed for the nonce into
an amateur Paul Revere, "booted and
spurred," reined up at the door after an
equestrian tour of the city, in search of
absent members or knowledge as to their
whereabouts.    Until long after midnight,
coupés and carriages flew around the corner, and drew up at the door of the armory
with a crash, which was followed by ring
of steel as the bayonets of the quadrupled guard unlocked and locked again,
admitting to the hall new-comers, as full
of curiosity as is natural in men summoned
suddenly from a summering by lake or
ocean side, and called upon to exchange
the touch of soft hands in gentle dalliance
for a grip of steel and readiness for stern
work.

Many had good cause to wear the faces
of knights of the rueful countenance, but

none did. To a set of business and professional men and clerks, called from com-
fortable homes in the city or in the
cool suburbs, the intolerable heat of
midsummer in a suffocating armory, without beds or bedding other than that pro-
verbial and much-sought "soft side,"
which a plank is popularly supposed to,
but rarely does, possess, might well have
been appalling, or at any rate irritating.
The period over which this confinement
might extend was also pleasingly indefinite,
and in many cases, doubtless, involved
serious questions of personal and professional engagements, likely to be broken at
no small cost. Not a man of them, however, seemed to give such considerations a
moment's thought. The appearance of
every new-comer was hailed with accla-
mations of delight, and he invariably
doffed his citizens' dress, and donned his
uniform in the enthusiasm of the moment, only to follow the example of his

predecessors in a few brief moments, during which it might be proper to say, metaphorically, that his enthusiasm was cooled, and reduce his habiliments to a minimum. But to say literally that anything or anybody in that armory was cool, cooled, or cooling during the ensuing four days, would be mendacious, to say the least.

All through the night the "boys" came pouring into the armory, singly and in twos and threes. Each man, after eagerly asking the regulation question, "Are we to go away?" and receiving the stereotyped answer that no such orders had been as yet received, had his own story to tell. Some had been out late, and found their orders upon a return home at an early hour in the morning; these, as a rule, found their explanations superfluous, the facts were axiomatic. Others had come in by late trains, some by milk trains from summer resting-places by the Hudson, or in the cooling everglades of

Jersey, or the sandy beaches of Long Island.

Later arrivals came from Newport, Long Branch, Lake George and Saratoga. These had in not a few touching instances been rudely recalled from dreams of love to deeds of war, and could be found in corners far, or as far as it was possible to get, from the "madding crowd," conning over delicate missives, written in the Anglo-Boston hand, or pouring into the ears of their sympathizing and confidential friends the tale of their interrupted summer romance.

It is not only fair to suppose, but it may in some instances be recorded as a fact, that the startling cry, which the W. U. T. and the A. & P's instruments emitted at their termini, "To arms, to arms," led many of the boys to arms, which they were loth to leave precipitately. In these instances, their tardy wooing had reached a climax precipitated by feminine fears of

danger to the knights summoned thus suddenly from carpet to field.

It can hardly be said that the armory
became quiet at any time during the
night. At the regular intervals the guards
were changed, and this made some noise,
while sleep did not come easily to the eye-
lids of many of the members unaccustomed
to overcoats for pillows and blankets for
beds on a night when coolest linen soon
became heated and uncomfortable.

The atmosphere of the armory was
superheated by numberless gas-lights
and by the presence of so many hundred
human beings, to a point almost beyond
endurance; but the boys, instead of growl-
ing, rambled about, chatting, and here and
there poker parties were organized.

## II.

SO THE watches of the night wore on, and the men were astir early in the bright midsummer dawn. Washing facilities were in great demand, but scarce. The matter of toilet did not, however, deeply concern their minds, which were much more exercised over the important question of breakfast. Where and how was this to be obtained? The commissary, however, proved equal to the occasion, and the boys were marched out in squads to breakfast at neighboring restaurants, with whose proprietors arrangements had hastily been concluded.

Among so many men there was to be found, of course, a variety of talent and accomplishments which could be turned to account in the way of divertisement for the multitude who, less favored, could only contribute their quota of energetic seconding and enthusiastic appreciation of the fun. Beginning in the company rooms, the spirit of mirth soon became general throughout the regiment as the men took advantage of the unusual opportunity for cultivating the acquaintance of comrades in other companies whom they were not in the habit of meeting on drill nights. The " gags " of each company soon became the property of the regiment, and as they met with general favor, could be heard in all parts of the building.

The "Seventh Regiment Sky-rocket," as the boys call it, consists of a unanimous whistling sound, a tremendous explosion, and the anxious sigh of gratification likely to assist at the successful termination of any rocket's career. The sounds are something like this :

"Swish-h-h-h—(prolonged). Boom ! —Ah-h-h-h," and when emitted in concert are startlingly realistic.

This was kept going with really wonderful pertinacity and enthusiasm; the men in all parts of the building picked up the "cue," no matter how frequently or from what quarter it was received, and kept "whooping her up" with a will. Gradually it seemed as though the men were becoming fairly intoxicated with excitement, and their unfailing flow of animal spirits incessantly bubbled over like champagne. Higher and higher rose the tide of innocent revelry, until fun held high carnival in all parts of the building as the hours wore away.

The day was if anything even warmer than its predecessor, and the broiling sun beat down upon the roof above the main drill-room, making the armory hotter than a furnace. As the sun moved away on its daily round, many of the boys sat out on the cornice under their second-story windows, smoking and cocking up striped-stockinged feet at all the world. The armory was rigidly guarded both as to egress and ingress, written passes being in all cases required. People passed without stopping much to look up. Eight hundred men were shut in there by evening, large re-enforcements arriving constantly, and a more happy, high-spirited crowd it would be difficult to find. Colonel Clark sat in his little office, which commands the main hall, and viewed the scene with the greatest pride and amusement. The favorite costume was a pair of trousers and an undershirt without sleeves.

When dinner-time arrived, Delmonico's waiters came hurrying in with big baskets and trays, and long tables were set in the large drill-room, and the men were marched in to a cold lunch of meats and

bread and iced coffee. The arrival of the
waiters was hailed with demonstrations of
unbounded joy by the hungry crowd, who
gave vent to a display of vocal pyrotech-
nics which greatly disturbed the imper-
turbability of the statuesque French *gar-
çons*, whose Gallic oaths, not loud, but
deep, gave indisputable evidence of their
lack of appreciation of American humor.
At 7, a similar meal was served to them,
which, as one of them said, " was n't such
d——d variety, but it tasted good." The
howitzers were taken into the drill-room,
and the men drilled in their use, and, with
one thing and another, the day wore away.
Watching the horse-cars was one of the
standing amusements, but the game
of draw-poker, according to Minister
Schenck's rules, was the chief. In the
officers' parlor was the head-quarters of
all the fun. At least three hundred men
were assembled there that night, ranged
about the piano in a semicircle ten deep,

and singing and dancing with great gusto.
"Way down on the Swanee River" was
called for. Immediately a young man in
a skeleton of an undershirt volunteered a
solo. His voice broke on the second
note, and a derisive shout settled him. A
score of suggestions were volunteered,
and in a second all was drowned in a
"sky-rocket," which was given with a
will. "The Sailor Boy" and the Gen-
darme song to original words met with
great favor, and for a double clog which
was volunteered, every man beat time or
"spatted" until the roof rang with the
tumult.

From the invisible treasure-house which
yielded all the necessary material for for-
warding the sports of the day, some one
drew a set of boxing-gloves, which at
once became the center of attraction for
the party. Invitations to "knock a chip
off my shoulder" were responded to by
inquiries as to "who struck Billy Patter-

son ? " It was not long before a match was arranged with much hilarity and no little facetiousness in regard to the terms and stakes. Suggestions as to the desirability of " steaks," which had been conspicuous by their absence from the day's bill of fare, were received with groans for the unfortunate punster, and a suggestion to " put him out " was gravely carried into effect before time was called for the boxing, which then began.

The general physical standard of the Seventh Regiment is very greatly misunderstood by the country at large. The fact that the regiment is largely composed of merchants and professional men who do not earn their living by manual labor is as widely known as is the name of the organization, and this fact has, not unnaturally, led many persons to suppose that the men would not be very formidable adversaries to cope with, were it not that intelligence and pluck more than made up for that supposed deficiency in "fighting weight." The fact is, however, that a very large number of the men, while they are not, it is true, physically developed by daily manual labor, are the very first among New-York's amateur athletes, almost every athletic, boat, and yacht club and gymnasium in the city being represented in the regiment. Any one who saw them rambling around the armory by scores in sleeveless gauze shirts, and marked the strong muscular backs and shoulders, well-developed arms, and the play of the muscles under the clear, healthy-looking skins, surmounted by clean-cut heads and bright, intelligent, manly faces, would have learned that brawn as well as brains enters largely into the composition of New-York's crack regiment.

Two of these athletic fellows proceeded to pummel each other lustily with the gloves until they were both exhausted, evanescent witticisms and facetious remarks of an encouraging nature being showered upon them by the crowd of bystanders even more thickly than were each other's blows. Other contests and "set-to's" followed, and the crowd, toward midnight, dropped off to their respective company rooms.

It was on this memorable day that an event of no little moment occurred. The name of the inventor of the great Seventh Regiment conundrum is, unfortunately, lost to the world. The origin of the immortal query is wrapped in mystery as deep and impenetrable as is the authorship of the Letters of Junius or the origin of species. That this will be a matter of as keen regret in the future to the historian and the antiquary as it is at the moment to the reader and the writer there can be little doubt. It will always, however, be a source of pride and gratification to its originator, whoever he may be, and he will undoubtedly feel *in articulo mortis*, to paraphrase the late A. Ward, that he has not lived in vain—but in New-York. At a time when there was a momentary lull in the storm of jollity, a voice from some quarter of the room shouted out the conundrum, " WHO WAS GEORGE WASHINGTON ? " This elicited from a score of near-by and evidently sapient throats the answer, in a school-boy's sing-song, " *First in war, first in peace, first in the hearts of his countrymen,*" which was immediately followed by a breakdown danced with the greatest vigor, the audible result being something like this : *Slam i tee slam bang, bang, bang !* For an instant there followed the hush of pleased astonishment, and then, with a roar of delight, the regiment made a rush in a body toward the quarter from whence the sounds described had proceeded. It was, although perhaps open to the objection of being, like all true American humor, slightly irreverent, a stroke of genius. In five minutes it had been repeated as many times, new voices each time swelling the choral response and twice as many additional feet assisting at the break-down, until the roof rang with the sound and the floor trembled under the repeated shocks.

The regiment had adopted the gag as its very own.

From that time forth there was hardly an hour of the day, nor even of the night, that this conundrum was not asked, and answered a score of times by grinning hundreds. It became thereafter the key-note to all the festivities during the encampment.

Again, the "head devils" of the regiment made night hideous, notwithstanding the good-natured growls of the sleepy-heads.

# III.

WEDNESDAY morning broke at last, bringing with it that undefined sense of impending danger which makes the air at times portentous, but it produced little effect upon the boys. The scene was changed a little, and the officers' assembly room, in which the previous night the boys disported themselves, bore the sign "Brigade Head-quarters," and had been taken possession of by Brigadier General Varian and staff. A guard was mounted over the door to keep out intruders, which added another warlike element to the scene. There was a prospect of work to do that night, but no indication of the fact could be found anywhere in the armory.

Breakfast was a little variation of the monotony of Tuesday's bill of fare, and consisted of eggs, rolls and coffee. After that important ceremony, Companies B and I drilled together as one company in the large drill-room, making an imposing show of seventy-five files front. They drilled *sans* jackets, and the movements of loading and firing and charge bayonets and charging on the advance were executed with the precision of clock-work. During this drill a catastrophe of a most serious nature occurred. Mr. Delmonico declared when called upon to feed the regiment that the " boys " should have the best of everything in his house, and accordingly the finest French china and cut glass were provided for their use. When the drill was in progress the waiters were requested to move the table on which these articles were, and in so doing they upset the frail structure, and demolished seven or eight hundred plates and goblets. The crash was frightful, and brought every man in the armory to an "attention." The usual card-playing was, however, soon resumed, and draw-poker passed away the time quickly for its devotees. Whist parties were made up and sought to rival it in attractiveness, but without success. Watching the horse-cars from the airy second-story windows and spinning yarns passed away the time for some, while the howitzer squad spent a good deal of time in familiarizing themselves with the use of their guns. "Rushing," as it is commonly known, was indulged in to some extent by the irrepressible fellows overflowing with animal spirits, and the query, "Who was George Washington?" which, ever and anon, rang through the hall, was sure to elicit the usual response, chanted forth by several hundred throats. A squad of the Eighth Regiment men, who were left

4

behind on the departure of that regiment for the north, were greeted with loud cheers as they marched in to report at brigade head-quarters.

During the day, Justus Schwab, the red-flag man, who was to preside at the Tompkins Square meeting that night, paid a visit of inspection to the armory on the invitation of a friend in the command. He had but little to say, and while he was sharply eyed by the boys, with a rare sense of humor, they gave, in his honor, as a rousing chorus, " The Son of a Gambolier." The words of that classic song are regimentally adapted ; the first verse (of an unlimited number) and the chorus are as follows :

" I 've been in ev'ry country,
I 've seen the soldiers drill,—
The Horse Guards of Victoria,
The Footmen of King Bill,
The Musketeers of bloody Spain,
The Cuban volunteer ;
But the Seventh of New-York 's the corps
For this Son of a Gambolier.

CHORUS:

> Then combine your humble ditties,
> As from tavern to tavern we steer;
> Like ev'ry honest fellow,
> I drinks my lager-beer,
> Like ev'ry jolly fellow,
> I takes my whisky clear;
> I 'm a rambling rake of poverty,
> And the Son of a Gambolier.
> Oh! I 'm a son of a — son of a — son of a—
> Son of a — son of a Gambolier,
> A son of a—son of a — son of a — son of a—
> Son of a—son of a Gambolier.
> Like ev'ry jolly fellow,
> I takes my whisky clear;
> I 'm a rambling rake of poverty,
> And the Son of a Gambolier.

The great German Communist failed to appreciate the humor of the song which " the boys " caroled forth right joyfully, but his eye noted carefully the appearance and the quiet look of determination under the smiles on the faces of the men, and he departed with his respect for New-York's citizen soldiery, as typified by the Seventh, visibly increased.

There was no lull in the fun during the day, although the older men speculated considerably upon the chances of their seeing some hot work in more senses than one that night.

Meantime, the authorities were not idle, and all was activity and subdued excitement around police head-quarters in Mulberry street and the head-quarters of the First Division, where for the moment the scene is located.

General Smith called together the Board of Police Commissioners in the morning, and, after a protracted consultation with his colleagues, sent the following communication to the Mayor:

POLICE DEPARTMENT OF THE CITY OF NEW-YORK, 300 MULBERRY STREET,
New-York, July 25, 1877.

*To His Honor Smith Ely, Jr., Mayor of the City of New-York.*

SIR: The Board of Police of the City of New-York, at a meeting thereof regularly convened at the Central Office of Police in said city on this twenty-fifth day of July, 1877, duly passed the following resolutions:

*Resolved,* That this Board, by reason of the disturbances and riots in other cities of this State and of the United States, and of threats of like riots and tumults in this city, apprehends a riot, tumult, and mob within the limits of this municipality, and that it therefore demands of and from the commanding officer of the military of the First Division the assistance of such military, to wit: Of the regiments known as the Seventh, Twenty-second, Eighth, and the Seventy-first regiments of said First Division, pursuant to the statute in such case made and provided ; and

*Resolved*, That the President of this Board request the written approbation of His Honor the Mayor of the City of New-York to the foregoing resolution, and to the demand therein contained, and that the President of this Board, after having obtained said approbation, serve a copy of the foregoing and of this resolution upon said commanding officer of the military of the First Division, and for a demand of the military assistance hereby required. I remain, sir, your obedient servant, W. F. SMITH.

To this Mayor Ely sent the following answer and indorsement :

*President of the Board of Police :*
I hereby approve of the resolution of the Board of Police demanding the assistance of the military of the First Division and of such demand.

SMITH ELY, Jr., Mayor of New-York.
City Hall, July 25, 1877.

Upon the receipt of the Mayor's written

approval, General Smith addressed the following note to General Shaler:

*Major-General A. Shaler, Commanding First Division N. G. S. N. Y.*

SIR: Herewith I have the honor to transmit to you a copy of two resolutions of the Board of Police of the City of New-York, passed this day as and for a demand upon you as commanding officer for the assistance of the military of the First Division — to wit, the Seventh, Twenty-second, Eighth, and Seventy-first regiments — together with a copy of the approbation thereof of His Honor the Mayor indorsed thereon, the original of which said indorsement will be exhibited to you herewith. And I hereby request you, on behalf of the Board of Police, to retain the above-mentioned regiments in their respective armories, subject to the orders of this Board.

I am, sir, yours respectfully,

W. F. SMITH.

General Shaler promptly sent his answer in the following terms:

HEAD-QUARTERS FIRST DIVISION
N. G. S. N. Y.,
New-York, July 27, 1877.

*General W. F. Smith, President Police Department, City of New-York.*

SIR: I have the honor to acknowledge the receipt of a copy of two resolutions passed at a meeting of the Board of Police held this day, with the approval of His Honor the Mayor indorsed thereon, demanding the assistance of the Seventh, Eighth, Twenty-second, and Seventy-first regiments, and to say that it will afford me pleasure to comply with said demand, except that I shall be compelled to substitute the Twelfth Regiment for the Eighth, which is now en route for Buffalo.

The regiments named are now assembled in their respective armories, equipped for service, armed with breech-loaders, and each supplied with forty rounds of ammunition per man. The armories are located as follows : the Seventh Regiment at Tompkins Market; Twelfth, Broadway and Forty-fifth street; Twenty-second, near Sixth avenue, in Fourteenth street; Seventy-first, at Broadway, corner of Thirty-sixth street.

These regiments will be at once directed to hold themselves in readiness to respond until further orders to any demand which may be made upon them by the Board of Police to aid in suppressing riot, tumult, or disturbance of the public peace, and to obey such orders and instructions as may be received direct from said Board of Police or its President.     Very respectfully yours,

ALEXANDER SHALER,

Major-General.

He then issued his orders to the commanding officers of the various regiments designated, substituting, however, the

Twelfth Regiment for the Eighth. The Eighth, it will be remembered, had already gone to Buffalo, a fact which the Police Commissioners, in the excitement of the moment, seem to have forgotten. Those received by Colonel Clark were as follows:

HEAD-QUARTERS FIRST DIVISION
N. G. S. N. Y.,
New-York, July 25, 1877.

*Commanding Officer Seventh Regiment.*

SIR: The Major-General commanding the division directs that you hold your command in readiness until further orders, to aid the police authorities in the suppression of riot, tumult, or disturbance of the public peace, and that you obey to the best of your ability such orders and instructions given for that purpose as you may receive direct from the Police Board or the President thereof.

Respectfully yours,

CARL JUSSEN,

Colonel, Division Inspector and Assistant Adjutant-General.

With the other preparations made by the Police Department this story has little to do. It is germane to the subject, however, in order that the reasons why no trouble actually occurred may be understood, that they be briefly alluded to.

The entire detective force was on duty, and a part of them were scattered through the disaffected quarters of the city east of the Bowery and west of Eighth avenue, in order to feel the pulse of the dangerous elements, and learn their plans if they had formed any. This, it appears, they had not done, and it soon became evident that the danger to be confronted consisted only in the readiness with which large gatherings of excited men are inflamed into a spirit of violence.

Arrangements for massing the police force at the entrances to Tompkins Square and for conveying re-enforcements to that place from the various precinct station-houses in omnibuses in waiting for the purpose, and other details suggested by previous experience were carefully attended to, and the knowledge of the facts widely disseminated, with a view to intimidating the mob. That it had the desired effect was afterward clearly demonstrated.

To return to the Seventh Regiment Armory. The supper hour arrived, and the meal was as noisily and hilariously discussed as had been its predecessors.

After it was concluded, Colonel Clark called together the regimental staff and the commanding officers of the companies, and announced his plans, which are now made public for the first time.

The record of the regiment at the Creedmoor rifle ranges was called into requisition, and the names of the men in each company who had acquired the greatest skill as marksmen were taken from the roll. These were to be detailed, and stationed as follows : a platoon to precede the regiment, and another to bring up the rear ; two men to be placed on the right and two on the left of the line of each platoon. These men were to be entrusted with the power to fire without orders, and were to keep a sharp lookout for persons in windows, on house-tops, or in the crowd, who should fire upon, hurl stones, or project any dangerous missile at the regiment. Any person detected in such a demonstration they were ordered to shoot down at once—and not to miss their aim. The remainder of the regiment was to await the order to fire.

These orders, while they may at first glance appear hazardous in the extreme, from the danger of one of the detailed men losing his head and precipitating an attack by a reckless shot, have been pronounced by able soldiers, experienced in street-fighting, as a masterpiece of strategy.

Street-fighting is acknowledged to be most trying to the nerves and courage of even the most experienced veterans, and it becomes doubly so at night.

A fair field, and the enemy in front,

usually test men's courage. How much more trying, therefore, is the venture into the streets where the enemy may be, and usually is, lodged on the house-tops, in windows, and behind trees, from whence to hurl a stone, or fire a shot unseen, into the ranks of a regiment.

At the conclusion of the council of war in Colonel Clark's little office, it was 7.30 P. M. Already the crowd had begun to assemble in Tompkins Square, but the Seventh boys were smoking their after-dinner pipes and cigars; groups were caroling forth music-hall ditties; the devotees of "draw" were at their favorite game of poker, and the spirit of deviltry was rampant throughout the large building.

"Rat-a-tat, rat-a-tat, rat-a-tat, rat-a-tat-tat, tat-tat-tat. R-r-r-r-r-r-r-r-r-r—r-r-r-r-r-r-r, rang out the sharp clear rattle of the drums.

In an instant, the careless, happy boys, the echo of whose laughter had hardly yet died away, became soldiers, ready for work.

Rapidly and quietly they gathered their accouterments, and fell in, each company in its room, and as each marched out, and took its place in line, three hearty cheers were given for the " Old Seventh." The deep affection of the men for the regiment, their enthusiasm, and their determination to uphold its honor to the death, rang out in those cheers, and a tear glistened in many an eye as the last echo of the " Tiger " died away among the rafters. Then all became quiet in the ranks, and the men stood firm and waited orders.

Forty rounds of ball cartridges were served out to each man, and they were directed to keep as quiet as possible, and to be ready to fall in at a moment's notice. Especially were they enjoined to keep away from the windows, and avoid show-ing themselves to the people in the street below. In case any thing was said to

5

them, or any stones or missiles were hurled through the windows, they were ordered to retire from the company rooms to the main hall, and not to make any demonstration in return under any circumstances. The men then broke ranks quietly, and awaited further orders.

The succeeding two hours were spent in quiet but restless excitement. The scene was in striking contrast to that of the previous evening, when the boys were skylarking at will. They wore serious faces, and evidently realized that this was serious business. All were in a state of the most unenviable uncertainty.

Among those in uniforms were many members of the Veteran Corps, who had reported to the commanders of their old companies for duty, and voluntarily and quietly taken their places in the ranks, for the purpose of standing by the honor of the " dear old Seventh."

Many of the younger men were all

anxiety for the order to come which should send them out to smell powder for the first time.

"Gim'me another bucketful of gore," was their cry, in an under tone.

With the men who had seen service before during previous riots, the feeling was very different. They were quietly determined, and quite prepared to go out if it became necessary for them to do so, but they were far from anxious. They knew from former achievements that it was by no means amusing. That there is little glory and less comfort in having one's head crushed by a brick-bat they had learned by experience. In the event of trouble, they knew too that the force of their example would be beneficial in keeping the new men up to their work, so they stretched themselves upon the floor, and rested upon their arms.

A longer two hours men rarely know than these which the boys so quietly passed. They were not even called upon to follow the orders about self-control in case of hostile demonstrations from without. The street below was quiet as midnight; its silence only broken at short intervals by the tinkle of the bells on the car-horses as the cars passed emptily along. Yet the air was full of apprehension. Occasionally there would be heard a sound like a faint cheer, and the men lying on the ground would raise themselves on elbow to listen, then all would be silent again, and they would fall back, pull their caps over their faces, and be at rest again.

Several scouts meanwhile had been quietly inspecting the scene of the expected disturbance. They had been selected by Colonel Clark for their experience, coolness, and good judgment, and in citzens' dress, dispatched at an early hour to Tompkins Square. Shortly after nine o'clock they returned, and reported what was soon known by word of mouth throughout the city.

The majority of persons composing the crowd which had assembled in Tompkins Square were workingmen drawn thither more by curiosity than real interest. The dangerous element, cowed by the ample and careful preparations made for their reception on the part of the authorities, civil and military, thought it best and safest to remain away.

The demagogues upon the platform made speeches which were meant for fire-brands to be hurled among an infuriated rabble. They fell upon unsympathetic ears, and sounded like "buncombe." The crowd dwindled away, the communist leaders wrangled among themselves, blamed each other for the evening's fizzle with school-boy-like crimination and recrimination, and the meeting was over.

A few evil spirits made a disturbance at one of the exits from the square.

Whack, whack, whack descended the mighty service clubs of locust wielded by able-bodied policemen alike upon the heads of the just and the unjust, but the disturbance was "nipped i' the bud." The much-dreaded communist meeting was over, and the continued peace of the city fairly well assured.

Informal notice of the fact that the meeting had quietly dispersed was given the men, and in a moment the armory became again a bedlam. With a roar the pent-up feelings of the men broke forth like the mighty rush of waters which had borne down an impeding dam. The hot jackets were stripped off, pipes lighted, card-playing resumed, and those choice spirits, the "head devils," were soon busy concocting schemes to drive away that sleep which "knits up the raveled sleeve of care." The fatigue

which followed the excitement and sus-
pense of the evening added many to the
list of would-be sleepers that night, and
the watches of morning found the building wrapped in slumber, if the room of
the tenth company, which was never
quiet, be excepted.

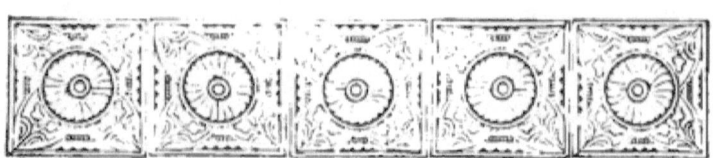

## IV.

THURSDAY morning dawned with the same white, hot sun rising in the same pale sky out of which the sun seemed to have scorched all the color. The air pulsed with the intense heat, but still the boys came up smiling, and were rewarded by hard-boiled eggs for breakfast, a relief from the monotony of Delmonico's delicate sandwiches and delicious iced coffee.

Many of the men had not stepped foot out of the armory since Monday night, but there were no signs of weariness nor any disposition to complain. They said, on the contrary, that they were just getting used to the life, and were willing to stay as long as they could be of any use.

Outside the walls of the armory the city was still very quiet and deserted-looking for New-York, even in midsummer. The Police Commissioners met and fanned themselves, congratulated each other upon the bloodlessness of the work of the previous night, and passed the following resolution, which was sent to the head-quarters of the First Division, and thence transmitted to the commanding officers of the various regiments:

*Resolved*, That General Shaler be requested to communicate the thanks of this Board to the Seventh, Twelfth, Twenty-second, and Seventy-first regiments, N. G. S. N. Y., for their services while at the disposal of the Police Department, July 25, and that he be requested to direct the regiments named to remain in their respective armories subject to the orders of this Board until further notice, unless they should be relieved from duty by order of the Governor of the State.

In the armory, the boys kept the carnival of fun going all day long. Those men, whose business imperatively demanded it, were given a few hours' furlough by Col. Clark in the morning, and appreciated it. Only those who really needed the leave applied for it. For the rest, they were fairly bursting with animal spirits, and instead of being subdued by the intense heat and close confinement, like good soda-water, they only effervesced the more.

The great conundrum : " Who was G. W. ? " was asked and answered a hundred times, the boys seemingly increasing with each repetition of the answer in their appreciation of its exquisite absurdity.

Not satisfied with that, however, some one sung out from the midst of a crowd :

" Who was Ben. Butler ? "

" *First in war, first in peace, first in the hearts of his countrymen !* chanted a couple of hundred throats, and *bang, bang, bang,* went twice as many feet in the regulation break-down which followed.

Here was a new idea, and with characteristic avidity the crowd seized upon it, and bandied it about from mouth to mouth, hundreds of voices and more feet being ever ready with the response.

"Who was Fanny Herring?"

First in war! first in peace!! first in the hearts of *her* countrymen!!! came promptly from the grinning crowd.

"Who was Jay Gould?"

(Same answer.)

"Who was Bill Tweed?"

(Same answer.)

"Who was Madame Blavatsky?" from a youth of theosophical propensities.

That was too—too much.

"Put him out! Bounce him!" they cried, and bounced he was with equal gravity and promptitude.

So through a list of well-known names the favorite gag was kept going, yielding unmeasured fun to men, who had been men not long enough to be hardened but, still men in the fight for life and honor which the world brings, long enough to be glad of an opportunity to act like school-boys again.

The regimental sky-rocket, which had been for a time neglected by reason of the tremendous popularity of the new gag, " Who was G. W. ? " was at length resurrected, and the "Swish-h-h-h — BOOM — Ah-h-h-h," which is so exactly like the sound which accompanies a rocket's flight, alternated with the great conundrum. It was sent up countless times during the day, and cheer upon cheer rang through the old market until at least half of the men were speechless from hoarseness. An extra dinner in courses was served to them. Shortly after the conclusion of the meal, a procession issued from one of the company rooms, fantastically dressed and preceded by a band carrying toy drums and trumpets, and beating and blowing them lustily. A banner was borne by one of the men, inscribed " Jennic's Guard." They made the round of the hall amid the wildest enthusiasm.

The heat made the men thirsty. Countless buckets of ice-water were consumed from the cedar by means of tin cups. Ice-water taken alone in quantities is well known to be injurious, and this accounted for the frequency with which men were seen retiring to corners, and taking the chill off the water with something which they poured out of a black flask.

There are probably very few, if any, drinking men in the regiment, but still many of the boys, naturally enough, like a "nip" occasionally, and various were the schemes concocted to obtain it. Naturally the first thing hit upon was the very simple expedient of hoisting a flask upon a string from the hands of friends in the street below. This worked well for a time, until the Colonel placed a guard outside the building and put a stop to it. At the same time an order was issued, and

6

all the men going in and out were "sounded" for bottles by the guard. Notwithstanding these precautions, however, a few sober-minded young men managed to keep a well-filled flask in their lockers. How this was accomplished still remains a mystery, which, as it may again serve the boys a good turn at some future day, it would be ungenerous to attempt to solve.

From the tenth company room came a suggestion that "Polo" might be played in the big drill-room upstairs. The proposal took like wild-fire, and the regiment adjourned *en masse* to the scene of the sport.

Sides were quickly chosen, a member of the Westchester Polo Club explained the rules of the game, and a dozen brawny youths, with big bunches of muscle showing through their clear skins, were selected for ponies. The goals were placed at opposite sides of the room, a manager chosen, brooms provided to do duty as mallets, and, armed with these, the players were soon mounted on the strong and willing backs of their alleged ponies.

The manager called " Time" amid roars of laughter from the crowd, and tossed the ball, which was improvised from a towel tied up with a string, in the air. The official report of the game was as follows:

*First Game.*—Grand charge for the ball. (Wild cheering from the spectators.) First man makes a pass at the ball, burns his pony's ear with his cigar, and is thrown. Second player and his pony stumble over him and fall also. Meanwhile, other players make wild passes at the ball, which at length is knocked over the goal and out of the window. Players dismount amid great enthusiasm.

*Second to Twentieth Games.*—Same as first.

At the conclusion of the first game a voice cried out,

"What is Polo?"

"*First in War! First in Peace!! First in the hearts of its Countrymen!!!*" came the response, followed by unnumbered sky-rockets and wild cheers.

For an hour or more, polo proved sufficiently amusing to hold the undivided attention of the regiment. The players and the ponies panted from their exertions, and glistened with perspiration which sprinkled their play-ground as it dripped from their faces under the influence of such violent exercise, with the temperature at ninety-odd degrees in the shade. They tumbled over each other, they collided, and went down in indiscriminate heaps of strong, bare, brown arms and gray legs, they shouted, they filled the air with evanescent witticisms, and they sang. The hours flew by, and, wearying of polo, not a moment elapsed before helter-skelter down-stairs they ran, and in a few moments two hundred coatless braves were

in line as strikers, and, headed by a banner inscribed with the legend,

> NO MONEY.
>
> NO HASH.
>
> NO WORK.

they made the round of the armory, pick-
ing up recruits, and finally waited on
Colonel Clark, and presented him with an
address, in which he was informed that
the boys demanded $10 per diem and
four square meals.

Colonel Clark, who thoroughly enjoyed
the fun, made the boys a brief, good-
natured speech and beat a hasty retreat
to his snug little den under the stairs,
where for four days he sweltered good-
humoredly.

Supper-time found the boys with good
appetites, and, refreshed by their perform-

ances with " Del's " cutlery, they returned with great zest to the pursuit of pleasure under difficulties.

An amusing travesty of the Pittsburg riots, and the disgraceful rout of the militia, and an undress rehearsal of the meeting in Tompkins Square, filled up the hours for the noisy gang, while the elder men settled down to poker, and, in some cases, to a vain endeavor to woo the drowsy god.

# V.

FRIDAY morning dawned upon the city, and found the boys tirelessly happy, notwithstanding the appalling heat, and the fact that no definite prospect of release from confinement came with it. It was the fourth, and as it proved the last day.

At Division Head-quarters, a copy of the following resolution, passed by the Police Commissioners, was received:

"*Resolved*, That His Honor the Mayor be informed that in the opinion of this Board it is not necessary to continue on duty the Seventh, Twelfth, Twenty-second and Seventy-first regiments at their respective armories subject to the order of the Police Board. The Board takes this opportunity to express to His Honor the Mayor its appreciation of the desire of the several regiments named to co-operate cordially with the Police Department while under its order."

This, while it was a gratifying assurance as to the probability of the continuation of quiet in the city, brought no prospect of release to the men who had been ordered under arms by the Governor of the State. That they would be dismissed from duty until the Governor was assured that order had been restored to the entire State was not probable.

News from the absent Eighth and Ninth regiments was anxiously looked for by the Seventh boys. Colonel Scott, of the Eighth, sent down during the day merry telegrams to various officers. " Happy as a clam," " Lovely as a rose." From the Ninth, at Albany, the latest news was brought by ex-Colonel Braine, who had gone up with the regiment, and returned. He reported the boys in fine spirits, encountering the heats of July with fortitude.

Everything being quiet in the city, leave was granted during the day to many of the men to go to their homes and places of business for a few hours.

General Varian was still on duty in his head-quarters, which he had established in the officers' parlor, as he had been continuously from the start. Here the time had been passed in chatting, story-telling, and popping champagne corks. The time was shortened by the stories of the chief medical officer of the staff, who is acknowledged the best *raconteur* that New-York can boast. Occasionally, the uproar without would start all hands for the drill-room, to laugh at the boys' fun. By Friday, however, the staff officers grew weary, and half of them obtained leave, reporting for duty again, however, promptly at six o'clock.

At ten o'clock in the morning, Mayor Ely and the Board of Police Commissioners visited the armory, and were received by Colonel Clark. As soon as it became known that they were in the building, the boys prepared to give them a reception, and the company rooms were decorated. One company laid out as its coat-of-arms four aces and a king, surmounted by a whisky bottle rampant; another mounted a fine miniature battery of black ale-bottles. As the visitors passed from room to room the boys cheered vigorously, and finally informed them that George Washington, Esq., *was* first in peace, etc. The Mayor was very much amused, and requested to be shown a game of polo, an account of which he had read in the morning newspapers. The boys, nothing loth, made their preparations, and then His Honor was escorted by the " Jennie " Guards to the large drill-room, where a seat of honor, flanked by the regimental colors, had been provided for him. Several games of polo were played, and then the demands of the strikers of the night before were referred to the Mayor, who read them with huge enjoyment, after which he

went out amid a flight of " sky-rockets."
The armory then settled down to quietude.

Suddenly the following orders were
posted up in various parts of the building:

HEAD-QUARTERS CONTINENTAL GALOOTS,  
          New-York, July 27, 1877.

GENERAL ORDERS,  
    No. 19,000,000.

The Galoots will assemble this evening in
full regalia at the Adjutant's call, which will be
sounded at 9.00 G.M.

Field and Staff dismounted. No police. No
flowers.

The Telephone Corps will report to the Adjutant half an hour before the formation.

      By order of Col. WALTER S. WILSON.

W. A. LENTILHON,  
    Brevet Lt.-Col. & Adjutant.

(Official.)

" A Mock Parade ? "

" Yes "—was the query and answer,
which passed around. The signatures were
those of the two young men, members of
the tenth company, who had been the
foremost in all the deviltry of the three
preceding days.

A spirit of emulation was aroused, and each company began making its preparations for participating in the fun, and outdoing if possible its fellows in the absurdity of its costume, and the originality of its contribution to the general quota of amusement.

An offer of the use of the swimming baths, which was received, was communicated to the men, accompanied by permission to avail themselves of it should they like to do so. But they had other business on hand, and hardly a corporal's guard were lured by the offer of a swim, although it was a day to make a man wish himself amphibious. Later on a florist sent in, with his compliments, a superb flower piece of colossal size, containing as a device an American flag and the figure " 7." Some of the men found that the coping beneath the second-story windows was wide enough to hold a chair comfortably, and it was soon filled with a row of statues, after the manner of that of the late Mr. Seward.

All the afternoon and evening the doors of the company rooms opening on the main hall remained closed to every one but their own members, who ran in and out at intervals, and carried bundles and dispatched messengers with a delightful air of secrecy. It was quite evident that some event of unusual importance was on foot.

Mysterious packages, paint-pots and other unmilitary paraphernalia were smuggled into the company rooms, and the armorer and janitor was driven nearly out of his head by the demands made upon him for supplies unknown to him theretofore as being among the requisites of a first-class militia regiment.

Quiet reigned to such an unwonted degree that Colonel Clark anxiously poked his head out of the door of his little sanctum at intervals, and surveyed the deserted hall-way with a dubious smile. Finally some one called his attention to the orders quoted above, when he grinned and retired with a re-assured air to his office.

Supper-time arrived, the meal was dispatched hastily and in comparative silence, and the men beat a rapid retreat again through the firmly closed doors of the company rooms, where they remained until nine o'clock. Peals of laughter occasionally rang out from behind the closed doors, but the men were invisible.

A committee waited on Brigadier-General Varian and staff and Colonel Clark and the regimental staff, and invited them to the main drill-room on the floor above, where seats had been provided for them on a table, a number of civilians who had been invited down, or who had heard of the fun going on daily and nightly at the armory, were admitted by the Colonel's orders, and all was in readiness.

In a few moments the companies began to issue from their rooms and form in line. The reason for the closed doors and subdued bustle which had pervaded the company rooms during the day was at once apparent. The first company wore its regimental trousers turned inside out, and was naked from the waist up, and a gigantic figure " 7 " was painted in black on each man's bare breast, except that of the darky water-carrier, who was elegantly attired in a similar white-chalk figure. Another company appeared as Highlanders in blanket kilts. A third wore uniforms made of brown paper in the Continental style, with the inquiring legend on each man's back in large letters, " Who *was* G. W. ? "

Still another company was arrayed in large flour sacks, and one company was composed of stuffy-looking fat men. A battery was organized, and came solemnly upon the scene dragging by a ponderous harness a toy cannon about two inches long. The line was formed with about four hundred men. The crowd of spectators was kept back by a detachment burlesquing the "finest police force in the world," who plied their (stuffed) clubs with equal impartiality and vigor. The absurdity of the scene was heightened by the pride taken by the men, fantastically dressed as they were, in executing the orders they received with the same precision which distinguishes them when upon duty, and the line was as straight as it was all the way down Broadway in "61." The Colonel then took his place in front of the line with an enormous feather-duster plume in his cap, and with so many pairs of stockings in the breast of his coat that he greatly resembled a pouter pigeon. With much difficulty he folded his arms above this expansive breast and maintained an air of dignity so like Colonel Clark's that he was greeted with enthusiastic cheers and shouts of laughter from the audience. The Adjutant, who was dressed in a costume of decorative flags, and looked like a Bedouin Arab, then formed the parade in the most accurate manner, and read the following orders :

HEAD-QUARTERS CONTINENTAL GALOOTS,
NATIONAL GUARD, J. A. M. S. N. Y.,
CAMP HARDSCRABBLE, July 27, 1877.

General Orders,
No. 19,000,001.

*Paragraph 1.* In compliance with a general order received from Albany in a disgustingly sudden manner, about four minutes ago, this command will parade in night-shirts, without sleeves, at six inches past two o'clock, to-morrow (Saturday) morning. Captains of companies will see that their men are provided with twelve years' rations, consisting of the following, viz. :

1 Chromo of George Washington, with the usual conundrum attached.

17 Bologna Sausages.

1 Thumb Tack.

14 Tuns of Holland Gin.

8 Reinas, Hoboken Brand.

1 Sock, " Bill Heath " calibre.

93 Fish-Balls.

21 Nutmeg Graters.

1 Derrick.

1 Ounce of Minnie Gudgeons.

And, "in case of fire," one small "stash of fluid."

Each 1st Sergeant will see that his company is supplied with one cake of Soft Soap for purposes of occasional ablution.

*Paragraph 2.* There having been a land-slide in Skeneateles, which village is situated on the Harlem River, between Goose Creek and Podunk, four hundred miles from the Elysian Fields, and ninety-three inches from the dumping grounds, the Galoots will occupy the left bank of the aforesaid stream, and attend to the slaughter of the nimble potato-bug.

However, this is neither here nor there.

In crushing these riots, the betting is 100 to 60 that we are liable to receive the " grand cough " ; in consequence of which each and every man, without regard to sex, will furnish himself with a diving-bell and book of directions.

*Paragraph 3.* The Commandant will now go on to state that this is all; adding, however, parenthetically, that owing to circumstances of a suspicious nature, he has not tasted flesh for seventeen long years.

FLESH includes fluid.

He is now prepared to wallow in great lakes and lagoons of Rhenish wine. And for no cause.

*Paragraph 4.* Major Chas. Snively is hereby appointed Officer of the Day—for last night, and

handsome Badgely will be Officer of the Guard—
with a large copper.

By order of
Col. WALTER S. WILSON.

W. A. LENTILHON,
Brevet Lt.-Col. & Adjutant.

(Official.)

These orders were received with peals of
laughter, eliciting the stern command
from the flatulent Colonel:

"Silence in the ranks!"

The "beat-off" by the drum-corps and
band, who were equipped with drums of
tin wash-basins and toy trumpets, the
Drum-Major being a side-splitting carica-
ture of that gorgeous functionary, was
again cheered. When the command of the
regiment was turned over to the Colonel
by the Adjutant, that officer led out
and introduced "Governor Robinson," in
the person of an imposing and bald-headed
sergeant, who was dressed in a black
frock and an old-fashioned and gigantic
beaver. The "Governor" made a short

speech in the most approved stump-orator style, in the course of which he irrelevantly remarked several hundred times that "if there was one thing more than another that was it," and that, however, this was "neither here nor there" and "for no cause."

He finished his address by the statement that he would proceed at once to solve the Eastern question.

"Attention !! " yelled the alleged Colonel, and every man cleared his throat with an effect like the "grand cough."

The "Governor" solemnly removed the American flag which had been thrown over a flour barrel behind him, raised the barrel, turned it on end, and extracted from beneath it a small plaster bust of George Washington, which he gravely placed upon the bottom of the barrel, and removed his hat.

"Who was George Washington?" yelled the Adjutant.

Then, with a mighty roar from the nine hundred throats in the lines and the audience, came the response :

" First in War ! FIRST IN PEACE !! FIRST IN THE HEARTS OF HIS COUNTRYMEN !!! " And this was emphasized with a double-headed breakdown which shook the walls, and made the floors tremble mightily.

The lines having been opened, the alleged Governor inspected the troops, accompanied by the Colonel, Adjutant and Lieutenant-Colonel. The latter was extremely amusing in his dress, which was white, with two soda crackers for epaulets and two lemons for coat-tails, and he was obese to the last degree. He demonstrated the duties of his office by frequently wiping the Colonel's nose and giving him an occasional puff on his cigar. The Governor bowed blandly and inconsequently in every direction, and when introduced by the Colonel to the captains as they passed, immediately grabbed and fervently shook the hand of the nearest private, after the manner of the machine politician. The artillery fired a salute for the Governor, the building shaking with the detonation of the piece, which made a sound like a small fire-cracker.

Then the men were put through the manual of arms and the battalion drill. The precision of their movements under the voluntary command of some of the youngest men in the ranks spoke volumes for the efficiency of the regiment, and pleased Colonel Clark greatly. The spectators were aroused to so great a pitch of enthusiasm that cheer after cheer rang out as the men executed difficult movements, and culminated, when, after a marching salute to General Varian, the parade was dismissed, in a mighty yell of delight.

The fun reached a climax in that memorable "shindig" just in time.

An hour afterward, "Camp Hardscrabble " was broken up by order of the Governor of the State.

The order disbanding the New-York militia reached the Seventh Regiment Armory about 11.30 o'clock. Some of the men had gone to bed, but the majority were still engaged in their evening revelry. The order was passed around, but it did not create a great amount of feeling one way or the other. While many of the elder and more staid members were glad to be released and to return to their homes, some of the younger received the order with apparent regret. Then there was lively bustling throughout the company rooms as the men hastened to change their regimentals for their civilian costumes. The ammunition which had been issued to the boys was returned and accounted for, after which the regiment was disbanded by companies. The men performed these duties in a quiet, business-like manner, the only sign of enthusiasm being manifested as each company was dismissed, when three cheers were given. The men were allowed to take their knapsacks to enable them to unpack such articles as had been placed in them in anticipation of a possible transfer to some other part of the State. So for an hour or two, well-dressed young men were seen carrying knapsacks through the streets adjacent to the armory, making their way home by devious routes. Now and then they were jeered by corner loafers, but no notice of this was taken, and the streets were soon as quiet as ever. Colonel Clark sat in his room in the armory half an hour after the order had been read. He leaned back negligently in an easy chair, and it could easily be seen that a burden had been lifted from his shoulders. "I felt that the responsibility resting upon me was great," said the Colonel. "My anxiety did not arise altogether from the anticipation of an impending riot and its effects upon the city; I felt the responsibility of handling my men with discretion in case such a thing did happen. A large proportion of them are young, and have mothers," said he, feelingly, "and had any of them been killed there is no knowing where the blame would have been placed. But since Wednesday night I have felt that the whole danger was over." Those of the men and officers who lived out of town remained at the armory over night.

When these departed in the morning, " Camp Hardscrabble " was broken up forever. Its memory will, however, last as long as any of the men who passed those four days in the armory shall live. More : it will be remembered by those who derived, in no small degree, a feeling of immunity from danger while the boys were camped down in the old Market. Men who know how to play know how to fight. They did not fight, they suffered only minor discomforts, but they were there, and behind them were the traditions of the regimental past, dear to the heart of every New-York man, woman and child, and thrice dear to " the boys " themselves.

" What is the Seventh Regiment ? "

" Now then, all together —— "

THE END.

# The World's Creed.

THE WORLD *believes the Enemy of Mankind may be trusted to attend to his particular business of stirring up strife. It therefore seeks to promote peace on earth and good will among good men.*

THE WORLD *believes that even the Moon has two sides. It therefore gives every honest man credit for supposing himself to be right, no matter how wrong it may hold him to be.*

THE WORLD *believes that sufficient unto each day are the evils thereof. It therefore considers it quite unnecessary to embitter existence to-day by fighting over the fights of yesterday.*

THE WORLD *believes there was some sense in the old superstition according to which every day's fortune was colored by the first objects seen in the morning. It therefore thinks that to lay on a man's breakfast table a sheet full of unclean things, angry words, personal squabbles and political spites, is about as likely a way of propitiating his good will as to put spiders into his coffee. As a mere matter of business, therefore,* THE WORLD, *endeavors to be fair to its opponents in politics, candid in its discussion of public questions, just to all men—and "up to the latest news."*

Since The World's Employment Office was opened on October 21, 1878,
11,988 Employers have been supplied with suitable servants.

REPORT OF

# The World's Employment Office,

## For the Year Ending Oct. 21, 1879.

| | Servants applied. | Servants admitted. | Servants placed. | Employers applied. |
|---|---|---|---|---|
| | 15,451 | 12,916 | 10,138 | 11,988 |
| Reregistered | 5,047 | 5,047 | ...... | ...... |
| Totals | 20,498 | 17,963 | 10,138 | 11,988 |
| Cooks | 2,805 | 2,434 | 3,102* | ...... |
| Chambermaids | 3,382 | 2,959 | 2,821 | ...... |
| General housework | 1,182 | 933 | 1,428 | ...... |
| Laundresses | 843 | 690 | 594 | ...... |
| Nurses | 1,562 | 1,366 | 1,026 | ...... |
| Waitresses | 324 | 286 | 375* | ...... |
| Ladies' Maids and Seamstresses | 286 | 272 | 120 | ...... |
| Miscellaneous—Females | 606 | 539 | 164 | ...... |
| Waiters and Butlers | 1,135 | 842 | 232 | ...... |
| Coachmen and Grooms | 1,184 | 813 | 117 | ...... |
| Miscellaneous—Males | 2,142 | 1,782 | 159 | ...... |
| Totals | 15,451 | 12,916 | 10,138 | 11,988 |
| Reapplied and admitted | 5,047 | 5,047 | ...... | ...... |
| Totals | 20,498 | 17,963 | 10,138 | 11,988 |

* Where more servants are shown as "placed" than are shown as "applied" it is
because some have had two or more places in the year and only applied once to register.

## THE WORLD

employs confidential Agents to investigate the character of those who wish to
advertise for situations or to register at its Employment office.

## THE WORLD

will not print the advertisement of any Servant who has not a good established
character. The fact that an advertisement appears in *The World* is proof that
the advertiser is an honest, trustworthy, sober, capable person.

No other newspaper in the city makes any inquiry as to the character of those
who wish to advertise for situations in its columns.

## THE WORLD'S EMPLOYMENT OFFICE

is clean and neat, the clerks in charge are competent, polite and attentive. It is a
great success and has become a necessity to housekeepers. When you are in
want of a servant, try it.

## The World's Employment Office,

### 1267 BROADWAY, & 634 SIXTH AVE.